Usborne
Phonics Readers
Frog on a log

Phil Roxbee Cox

Illustrated by Stephen Cartwright

Edited by Jenny Tyler

Language consultant: Marlynne Grant
BSc, CertEd, MEdPsych, PhD, AFBPs, CPsychol

There is a little yellow duck to find on every page.

First published in 2006 by Usborne Publishing Ltd., Usborne House, 83-85 Saffron Hill, London EC1N 8RT, England. www.usborne.com
Copyright © 2006, 2001 Usborne Publishing Ltd.

Frog sits on his log
by the bog.

With one big hop,
he jumps over
the bog.

3

Off he goes! Frog likes to jog.

"I'm a jogging frog
from the log
by the bog."

5

Frog's jogging has ended.
It is foggy.

Out of the fog
runs Pup the dog.

Pup can't see.

He bumps into Frog's log.

7

Frog is back up on his log. Along trots Big Pig in the fog.

Pig is looking for
Pup the dog.

Now he bumps into Frog's log...

Next day, it is sunny.

"Bump into my log!" says Frog.

Is Frog trying to be funny?

"Bump your log!"
barks Pup the dog.

"You will not call us silly dog and hog?"

"No, bump away!" croaks grinning Frog.
"I cannot fall off. I'm strapped to my log."

So Big Pig and Pup the dog bump into the log...

...which tips back into the bog...

...taking with it foolish Frog.

Frog is agog.

"Now it is me who is silly. A silly frog!"